Stirring up Some LOVE

Linda Boulanger

Stirring Up Some Love
A Wings & Whispers Love Story
©2018 by Linda Boulanger

Edited by Grace Augustine/Edits with a Touch of Grace
Cover Design/Interior Design by Tell~Tale Book Covers

Published by TreasureLine Publishing

Also available in eBook publication

PRINTED IN THE UNITED STATES OF AMERICA

I dedicate this book to my sister, Leigh,
my brother, Dean, and our Dad…
Cancer took you all well before your time.
Forever loved, forever missed.

To my husband, beloved warrior of God… battle strong.

And to all of you who fight this beast on a daily basis…
You each have a place and you all have my heart.
Be the storm.

FATE WHISPERS TO THE WARRIOR,
"YOU CANNOT WITHSTAND THE STORM."
THE WARRIOR WHISPERS BACK,
"I AM THE STORM!"

~author unknown

Chapter 1

La Boulangerie de L'amour.

Most days Felicity loved reading those words etched on the window of her little shop on Sweet Street. As an angel of love, she loved love and loved helping make it happen. But, that day as she walked up to her little love bakery, she felt her heart sinking. For the first time since she'd received her wings, Felicity was uncertain about her mission. She wasn't at all sure that her current client was the right bride for the groom.

The angel shook her head, her silky gold curls swishing about her shoulders. It really wasn't her place to decide. All she was supposed to do was add her special magic to the cakes to assure that the love between whoever took the first two bites would last a lifetime. That was it. Her mission was simple, it was romantic, and had never failed. But, she'd never *not* wanted to make sure a couple stayed together, either.

Felicity dropped her bags onto the work table in the back of her shop and plopped down on the stool. With her elbows on the table, she leaned forward, palms against the sides of her face, fingertips meeting at the tip of her forehead. She groaned and rubbed her eyes before steepling her fingers in front of her perpetually pink lips. What was she going to do?

Her job, that's what.

She pushed up from the table and stormed toward the vintage eight burner, double oven Wedgewood. She twisted the knobs, listening for the tell-tale click, click, click of the automatic ignition, only instead, it sounded like a tsk, tsk, tsk.

"Shut up!" Her arms crossed in front of her, she glared at the silent black behemoth.

With the corners of her mouth drooping, Felicity returned to her stool, grabbing a file on the way.

Chusi—Herensuge

When said together, the couple's last names sounded like the villain from a bad B-rated thriller. The bride, one Adelind Chusi, could have easily played a psychopathic murderer with her bride-from-hell tactics.

She's not THAT bad, her mind chided.

Felicity growled, a sound low and deep in her throat. She dropped the folder onto her work table and whipped it open. *TAKE 5*, it said in bold red letters across the first page.

"Oh yes," Felicity whispered. She really was *THAT* bad, and then some.

Thumbing through the pages, the corners of her mouth dropped when she came to the image she'd clipped from the newspaper of the *happy* couple's engagement photo. Neither smiled as the photographer captured them for all time. Poor Dirk. He must have hated that moment that bound him to the harpy. Not that she was a real harpy. Felicity had met a few of those birds of prey that most often had women's faces, and...

Oh, never mind, she thought. Dirk seemed to have

come to terms with the union since then, seeing how he was always so jovial when he and bridezilla visited her shop. He was always making jokes and trying to get the porcelain doll to crack a smile. They made Felicity laugh, funny or not, because she liked how much he seemed to appreciate her efforts. Besides, his humor made her giddy, and laughter always followed.

Thinking about the handsome dragon shifter made her smile. How he had managed to saddle himself with a serpent queen was beyond her. What wasn't beyond her was the ability to assure their love for one another for all time.

Head down, she let out a drawn-out sigh before pulling the recipe for the current cake she was going to make to try to please the bride. *Italian Butter Cream*. It wasn't a standard grooms cake flavor, but Adelind had taste-sampled everything else. If this didn't work... Felicity shook her head.

This. Would. Work.

The angel had already decided a pinch of magic was in store. She'd earned the right to use it, if only to save her own sanity. Not so much because of the unpleasable bride, but because she couldn't bear to see Dirk Herensuge anymore. Her heart was getting way too involved.

Chapter 2

Felicity brushed the last of the flour dust from her rosy cheeks when she heard the bell that signaled she had a customer. She glanced at the oversized, heart-shaped wall clock. 2:00 pm, on the dot. Blowing out a quiet breath, she attempted to still her heart and pasted on her best smile, whirling around to meet... just the bride.

"Adelind... er, Ms. Chusi."

Felicity glanced over the shoulder of the slender, dark-haired woman as she glided into the front part of her work area. Surveying the front of the store, the angel pursed her lips, and wrinkled her forehead. Evidently, they were to go it alone that day. She shrugged and turned toward the woman who had slipped past her to perch on the padded seat of one of the vintage soda chairs with the wrought iron, heart-shaped backs. Her well-manicured finger was already streaking through the frosting of the cake Felicity had placed in the center of the table.

Brows rising, Adelind looked at her as she licked the frosting from her hand. "What's in it?"

"It... it's Italian Butter Cream. There's cream cheese, bu... butter, powdered sugar, vanilla, coconut, and... chopped walnuts." Felicity held her breath as the bride-to-be went in for another taste.

Adelind nodded, her head bobbing up and down slowly. "This is... if the cake itself tastes half as good as the frosting…"

Felicity quickly cut a piece and thrust a platterful toward the bride to be, holding her breath while her tougher-than-ever customer tasted it.

Honest to God, the woman's eyes practically rolled back in their sockets, her lids fluttering as she threw back her head. "Mmmm. Oh, this is… Oh, yes. Yes. Yes."

Felicity's eyes widened and she stepped back from the table when the woman moaned again. Awkward only barely described how she felt. It was way too much like intruding on a… well, a private moment.

"Oh, Jordi is going to be so sorry he missed this." She licked her lips and smiled up at the angel. "Well, it's his loss for being late because I'm just going to make the decision without him. Done! Done, done, done. This is it. THIS is my choice for the groom's cake."

Letting go of the bottom lip she'd caught between her teeth, Felicity smiled. "I think you've made an excellent choice, Ms. Chusi. I'm sure Mr. Herensuge will agree wholeheartedly with your decision."

"With what decision? Did you finally make a choice, Adiebind?"

Both women turned toward the looming figure that had burst through the front door like the devil himself was after him. Except, the carefree smile that turned up the corners of his full lips told a different story. Dark blue eyes, crinkling at the corners, sparkled as Dirk Herensuge winked at the angel, and Felicity was certain her cheeks must have reddened two shades deeper.

"Sorry I'm late. What have I missed? Obviously,

something special to have gotten your stamp of approval, Grumpy."

"Oh, Jordi! Grow up! I swear, you're going to be late to your own wedding the way you galivant around with absolutely no respect for time."

Bridezilla waved off his eyeroll and motioned for Felicity to cut another piece of the sample cake. His fingers brushed the angel's when she handed it to him and she could have sworn he chuckled when she jumped, though his humor faded immediately when he took the first bite.

"Good Lord in Heaven," he groaned as he pulled the fork from his mouth.

Good Lord was right. Felicity wondered if she'd added too much magic because... and this was where she desperately needed Divine intervention... the man moaned, too. Merciful heavens, she stood staring at him, barely able to catch her breath, especially as he traced the contour of his upper lip with the tip of his tongue.

Before Felicity knew what was happening, her mind formed an image of the man's mouth and tongue on her in places she'd barely ever imagined someone touching her. Her eyes wide, she quickly shuttered her mind, remembering the groom was a Druajen. She knew from past experience that dragon shifters from that line had the ability to see into other's thoughts. In fact, that was how the couple knew she was an angel. She'd been floored when the groom announced that little-known detail during one of their early meetings. He'd chuckled when her mouth fell open.

"Druajen," he'd said, pointing to his temple.

She'd remembered, at that point, reading the

newspaper article of their engagement: *Oldest son of the Herensuge Druajens to wed the only daughter of the Serpent King.*

She bowed her head, praying she hadn't closed off her mind too late for him to know she'd been thinking mouth-watering thoughts about him, only to find him staring at her with a salacious glint in his eyes when she finally looked up again. *Whatever*, she thought, her brows drawing downward, much as the corners of her mouth. It wasn't like there was any way the man could not know how much he affected women. She was sure she wasn't the first to have those thoughts about him, nor would she be the last. He could deal.

Felicity cleared her throat, put on her best professional face, and smiled at Adelind.

"Italian Butter Cream for the grooms cake it is, then."

"It's perfect!" The bride beamed like a happy bride should.

"And delicious," the groom added. "Sinfully so." Dirk winked at Felicity as he artfully maneuvered the fork, and her attention, back to his mouth around that fork. Seconds later, Adelind landed a smack on his arm and he flinched away in feigned pain.

"Oh, Jordi. You're seriously incorrigible. Stop harassing the poor angel."

He made a face at his bride. "I'll stop when you stop calling me by that stupid name."

With her mouth going into an immediate pout, Adelind crossed her arms over her chest. "Come on now. You know you'll always be little Jordi Boy to me."

With a groan, *Jordi Boy's* chin planted against his chest. He shook his head and half snarled, half sighed. "Three more days," he ground out. Without raising his head, he cut his eyes to look at Adelind. Felicity could see his brows going up, but his mouth was already beginning to curve into a smile again that had both women smiling as well, though hers faltered after a few seconds.

Three more days and she'd be stirring magic into a cake to assure her clients a lifetime of love.

Chapter 3

La Boulangerie de L'amour.

Whistling an upbeat toon, the dragon shifter couldn't say he'd been unhappy when Adelind had requested he make an unexpected visit to the little angel's bakery. Sweet innocence wasn't usually his cup of tea, but there was something about the celestial hottie that got his blood boiling like no one he'd met in the past few centuries. In truth, he was tired of the glammed up and glitzed out know-it-alls who thought they could *teach him a thing or two*, or the hungry ones who could think of little else but getting him to put a ring on it. No thanks. Wedding bells weren't a tune he wanted to hear.

Now, the little bell over the door of the Bakery of Love... that was a sound he couldn't wait for. Innocence be damned, his body was humming well before he turned the last corner.

He chuckled. The thoughts his angel had been thinking when he and Adelind had visited the day before sure hadn't been filled with a whole lot of innocence. He wondered just what it would take to get her to let him turn her thoughts into reality. Jordi Boy had a serious hankering to see whether she tasted as sweet as she looked.

"Mmm, mmm, mmm," he mumbled just before he pushed through the front door.

Felicity's frown turned from concentration to surprise when the bell above her door rang letting her know someone had entered her shop. She hadn't been all that busy lately, since it was an off season for planning weddings.

Giving the Chusi—Herensuge bridal cake a quick one-eyed, cocked-head look, she sprinkled a last bit of Forever Unified dust over the section of cake the bride and groom would eat first. She'd already stirred some into the batter, but wanted to make double sure their union would last.

Felicity sighed and brushed her hands together, ignoring the magic particles that floated into her open water glass beside it. It didn't really matter anyway. She was immune to her own magic. She took a quick drink, then turned her attention to the front of her store.

"Mr. Herensuge! I... I certainly didn't expect to see you today." Felicity's heartrate soared at the site of the dragon shifter, especially when she glanced past him to see that he was completely alone. He chuckled when her brows lifted and her eyes rounded.

"Not glad to see me, huh, Ms. Love? Don't tell me I need an appointment to drop by. I mean, your sign said *open...*"

Shaking her head, Felicity waved her hands in front of her. "No, no. It's perfectly all right. I just... I mean... well, I..." She stopped talking and clamped her lips together for a few seconds, exhaling loudly when he chuckled again. "Is there something I can help you with, Mr. Herensuge?"

When his brow raised along with the corner of one side

of his mouth, Felicity was immediately sorry she'd asked. Thankfully, it was at that exact moment she noticed he had something in his hand. His eyes followed hers and he lifted the ceramic replica of the old castle that sat on the cliff overlooking the East end of Hernathea. Shaladorn Castle. It had been in the Herensuge family for centuries. That had been one of the first things Adelind Chusi had told her when they'd discussed the reception venue. The couple would, of course, be married in the castle's resplendent chapel with the reception following in the exquisite great hall.

Felicity wasn't invited to the wedding, so the likelihood of her seeing the renowned chapel was slim to none. She'd made arrangements to deliver the cakes at two o'clock for the evening wedding. Normally, she preferred to get them in a bit earlier, but Mrs. Herensuge, the groom's mother, had planned a bride's luncheon in the hall and it would take time for the staff to rearrange the room.

Adelind had thrown a fit about not wanting her guests to see how any of it would look before the reception. Okay, so Felicity didn't know for sure if she threw an *actual* fit, but she could presume it from the whiny disgust in the bride's voice when she'd called to request a time change for set up. Regardless, the angel was intrigued by the miniature castle in the groom's hand.

"This…" He held up the replica. "This is a wedding gift, crafted by Maerara Volyris…"

Felicity sucked in a loud breath, her hands raising to cover her mouth for a few seconds before she held them out toward the castle.

"May I?" she asked, her voice practically a whisper.

She accepted the piece from Dirk with such care and adoration that one might have thought it made of pure gold. To Felicity, holding artwork crafted by the great Volyris... never in her life had she imagined something so glorious. She could practically feel the old harpy's talent seeping from the surface beneath her hands. *Volyris*. Not only was he gifted, he was one of the rare true male harpies. He was a legend, both in what he was and in his artistic ability.

"This is divine," Felicity commented breathlessly.

The groom chuckled. "Well, it's going to look even more divine when it's included in your cake design." He nodded when her mouth fell open. "Yep. Adelbrain's request. She's asked that you work the castle into the groom's cake. Maybe wrap the dragon's tail around it or something." He hurried on, "That part was my idea, not hers." He shrugged when Felicity raised a brow. "What can I say? I'm no designer. It just seemed..."

Turning her back on him, Felicity walked toward the workspace of her shop, stopping at the oversized table and settling the castle as far into the middle as she could reach. There was no way she was going to be responsible for a genuine Volyris falling to a shattered death on the floor of her bakery. She pulled out the image she'd drawn up of the groom's cake, studied it for a few seconds and nodded her head.

"As long as she doesn't mind it sitting at a bit of an angle, I believe it would look perfect right about...." She sketched a rough outline of the castle cradled by the dragon's tail, her smile widening as she held it up and turned to show him his idea come to life.

Only she turned right into him since he'd been peeking over her shoulder as she drew it in.

"Oh! Mr. Herensuge. I…" Felicity squirmed in the tight space between him and the table. "I'm sorry. I didn't mean…"

"This is preposterously inappropriate."

Dirk chuckled when the exact words she'd been thinking tumbled from his mouth and caused her to still, her brows shooting up.

"Did you forget, little angel? I can read your thoughts." He tipped his head down to gaze into her rounded eyes, the process causing the tip of his nose to almost touch hers. "I also know you've been thinking about kissing me since the moment I walked in the front door."

Quickly shuttering her mind and giving herself a mental shake in the process, Felicity disagreed, making sure to barely shake her head so as not to accidentally make any more contact with the man just inches from her. She couldn't let that happen.

"Mr. Herensuge. Please. This is really all just a misunderstanding…"

The dragon shifter stared at her for a few seconds more, then pushed back and stepped away.

Felicity sucked in a shaky breath and ran a hand over her hair to smooth down the curls that were trying to spring free from her messy bun. She cut her eyes up at the groom and almost faltered at his confused look. She turned to see what he was staring at.

"Is… there something wrong with the cake, Mr. Herensuge?"

She looked from the bridal cake to him and back again, cocking her head to study the multi-tiered masterpiece. At least she'd thought it a masterpiece, what with the edible dragon scaling up the side, its tail artfully wrapped around the tiers, its head peeking over the top layer to gaze at the bride and groom. Frowning, she looked back at him.

"*My* dragon's a tad bit more coral than that," he said absently, almost in a changing of the subject kind of way.

"Coral?"

He nodded. "And gold. Gold highlights. Kind of like my hair." He pointed to the thick, dark waves.

Felicity had to squint to see it, but sure enough, there they were... the faintest hint of golden highlights.

"Well..."

She reached for her notes, her heart beginning to beat even faster at the thought of having made a mistake. That was the hardest part of the whole cake. There was no way she'd have the time to remake it. She scanned the words scrawled on the paper. Nope. Adelind had said dark pink with a hint of orange.

"I don't know that I can change it…"

He tore his gaze away from the cake and stared at her like she had traded her wings for horns.

"Why would you want to change it?"

When she finally managed to close her suddenly slack jaw, Felicity reached up to rub her fingers across her forehead. This man was a true quandary. She shrugged. It didn't matter anyway. Adelind had told her the colors, even picking it out from some frostings she'd mixed up as samples. She'd much rather disappoint the groom by having the color slightly off than to incur the wrath of Ms. Chusi. That was one position she hoped she'd never find herself in.

"So, does it taste as good as it looks?"

His voice jarred Felicity from her unpleasant thoughts.

"Hmmm? Oh, the cake?"

He nodded. "Or the frosting, rather. It looks delicious, kind of like a scrumptious, creamy cloud, but with... substance. You know?" He chuckled when his description made her pucker her face. "Not very poetic? I guess I could have said it looks salaciously enticing with exquisite peaks and delicate, delectable curves and swirls waiting for a nibble."

Felicity fought to swallow, trying to keep her breathing steady, especially as his eyes traveled down her, practically devouring every peak and curve. "Very poetic," she squeaked out. "Wou...would you like a taste?" Her cheeks flamed when he slowly raised both brows.

"Absolutely."

Dear Lord, his voice was as smooth as her frosting, rich and deep with a timbre that may as well have been fingers skimming down her bare back toward...

Stop it! What was happening to her? She'd never in her entire four hundred and eighty-seven years on Earth ever had such thoughts about another being. Okay, maybe never was a bit farfetched, but she'd certainly never had them about a client. She closed her eyes for a split second. Reminding herself that she was a professional, she opened them and smiled.

"By all means, Mr. Herensuge, you truly should have a sample. Though I must warn you, it's nothing like the

Italian Butter Cream you tried before. And I don't have any extra cake. It will just be the frosting."

"Not a problem. The frosting's my favorite part."

Why didn't that surprise her?

Chastising herself, Felicity reached for the pipette she'd been using to add the finishing touches to the cake. She chose the one with the white frosting, not wanting to draw attention back to the dragon's coloring and piped some onto a spoon she had laying on the table.

Handing it to him, she frowned at his frown.

"Oh, don't worry. It's clean. I thoroughly scour every surface before I begin…"

Dirk was already shaking his head, his ever-ready smile making its quick appearance. He pointed to the spoon, or more so to the frosting on the spoon. His smile widened, and he chuckled.

"Cute," he commented.

Felicity covered her eyes in embarrassment when she realized the shape of the frosting in the spoon. A long sigh escaped her.

The double hearts, one slightly overlapping the other… it was just something she did. Her clients always loved it. Her shop was, after all, La Boulangerie de L'amour—The Bakery of Love. She specialized in wedding cakes and happily-ever-afters. She wished her mind had not been shuttered at that moment so she would not have to explain, but as she began, he shook his head and popped the spoon into his mouth.

Felicity watched, knowing the exact moment the fullness of the flavor hit his taste buds.

"To die for," he groaned. "I knew it would be."

He held out the spoon for some more, chuckling again when Felicity made sure the sample was a blob instead of hearts.

"This," he said around the spoon going into his mouth, waiting until after he'd removed it to continue. "Is a match made in heaven... the frosting and I. I'm pretty sure I could devour this whole cake myself, just for the frosting. I can't imagine how amazing the cake will taste."

He looked at her with such admiration it made her blush even harder. "You, sweet angel, have a true gift. Your ability to bring heaven to earth in exquisite, bite-sized pieces is unprecedented. No wonder Adelind agreed when my mom suggested that we should use you."

The mention of the bride extinguished all the warm pricklies his poetic words had fired up.

"Thank you."

Felicity knew the return of her formal tone must have baffled him by the way he raised his brows. It didn't matter, he needed to go. She needed him to leave.

"I really must get back to work, Mr. Herensuge. The bride's cake is practically done, but I have to finish the major details of the groom's cake. Since the dragon will be the focal point, it requires much more attention than the first one, and there really isn't a lot of time."

"Really? How long does it take to create one of these masterpieces?"

Felicity stared at him for a few seconds, trying to gauge whether he was serious in his curiosity or simply vying for time. She decided to give him the benefit of the doubt, and since she'd already moved further away from him to avoid any unnecessary contact, what harm could it do? It wasn't like she didn't love talking about what she did, and that chance didn't come up all that often.

"I usually figure in two days per cake, though I already had everything done on this one except the fine details," she explained, pointing to the cake with the dragon scaling the side. "The base of the groom's cake is also finished. It's just the dragon that needs work. And, of course, now I need to add in the Volyris castle."

Dirk nodded. "That castle really is something else." He reached for it, making Felicity cringe. "He even added the windows." He chuckled and glanced at her. "This one..." He used his finger to circle one of the windows high in the West tower. "That's my room. That whole tower is mine, actually. My brother lives in the other... when he's home." He laughed again, though his look turned serious. "I think renovating the towers into separate homes and giving them to us was our parent's way of hinting that they wanted us tied to Shaladorn. So far, it's worked out... with me, at least. Not so much with my brother, though I'm guessing that's all about to change."

Felicity's confusion dissolved as her focus caught the hint of sadness in his words. She was surprised at how much it hurt her heart.

"It must be exhilarating living in such a grand old place so rich in history though."

Dirk shrugged. "Don't get me wrong. I love the castle and grounds. I love my family and our heritage, but sometimes I feel bound to it, you know?"

He gave Felicity a sideways glance and she nodded, even though she really didn't understand. She had no history other than what she'd created over the past few centuries with the gift she'd been given before being sent down. And really, that was more the history of others that she'd helped give their starts as opposed to her own.

With an all over shiver, Felicity shook it off, refusing the cloud of gloom that attempted to settle over them. Happiness, she reminded herself, was within the grasp of all... mortal or otherwise. It didn't take having history or ... or even love. Sometimes, it took work and a definite desire to possess it.

She looked at the man standing beside her work table staring at the miniature Volyris masterpiece. Once he and his bride had eaten her cake, he was sure to have both. Happily-ever-after... it's what she specialized in. It's what her magic made happen.

"One last taste," he announced, reaching for the pipette. "Then I'll be out off."

Felicity watched him, her breath growing shallow at the mere vision of his hand wrapping around the icing-filled bag. She nearly sighed as he lightly kneaded the smooth surface before giving it a firmer squeeze, the white substance spilling out to cover the tip of his pointer finger on his free hand. He stared at the imperfect mound before rubbing his thumb across it, though not enough to fully squish it.

"I guess your parents never taught you not to play with your food." Felicity chided, powerless to keep the breathiness out of her voice.

He raised a brow and chuckled. "Thankfully, no," he said, sliding closer to her. He lifted his hand to his mouth, his tongue flicking out to trowel a small fissure in the icing mountain. When Felicity's jaw unhinged, her mouth opening slightly, he closed the space between them even more.

"Want some?" he asked, placing his finger against her lips before she could answer with more than a whimper.

He groaned when he pressed and she pulled his finger into her mouth, her tongue caressing the underside as she sucked the frosting off. When she raised her eyes to meet his, he drew in a hard breath, so hard that it made him cough, breaking the spell wrapping itself around them.

"Oh, goodness!" Felicity pulled away from him. She stared, wide-eyed, for a few seconds before wheeling around and rushing to the sink. "I'll get you a drink…"

Even before the water stopped and she could be certain, she had a sick, sinking feeling. In the silence, her ears picked up the sound of gulping. Felicity closed her eyes and shook her head before turning back toward him. Sure enough, he was drinking from the cup on her work table… the cup that she'd been drinking from just before she went to the front of the shop… the cup that she knew, without a doubt, had particles of Forever Unified magic dust.

Oh, this was bad! Bad, bad, bad. Worse than the feelings she'd had about him. Beyond the fact that she hadn't wanted to be a part of assuring a happily-ever-after for him and Adelind. Even more troubling than the innuendo associated with having his finger in her mouth. No, this took the cake.

"Calm down," she whispered to herself. Maybe... maybe it wasn't as bad as all that. Maybe... She blew out a breath trying to soothe her jitters enough so that she could think. Okay, she knew that *she* was immune to the spell. And since she was, maybe it would null and void the effect on him. Yes, that's what had to happen. No big deal. She'd just send him on his way and everything would be just fine.

Pasting on her professional smile once more, she took a few steps toward him. "I really must be finishing up now, so if you'll excuse me, Mr. Herensuge..."

"Mr! Please. Mr. Herensuge is my father. Sometimes my brother. *Why* can't you call me by my name?" He smiled and Felicity knew she'd been right to have been alarmed, especially when his chuckle came out as more of a throaty purr. "You know when I really want to hear you say my name?"

Felicity shook her head, her eyes so large they were surely bugging out of her face, and yet he was still looking at her with such lustful adoration. It would have been funny if the situation wasn't so dire.

"When I say goodbye as you're leaving my shop?" she asked with a hopeful half-laugh.

"Funny." He lightly tapped the end of her nose with the same finger she'd had in her mouth not nearly enough minutes before. "Ah, sweet Felicity. Hmmmmmm. See how easily that rolled off my tongue. You know why?"

She shook her head, scrunching her face in fear of what he was going to say.

"Mmmmhmmmmhmm." He stopped and moved closer to her, tipping his chin down to where they were nose to nose. "Because I've been practicing it." His single raised brow brought a high-pitched titter from her that made him laugh. "You're surprised? Really?" He shook his head. "Oh, sweetheart. I've thought of nothing but you for so long now. In fact, I'm pretty sure I was thinking about you even before we met."

That comment took Felicity off guard. She'd heard some pretty aggressive pick-up lines, but that…

The phrase, *Saved by The Bell,* had never had a more poignant meaning than it did when the bell over her front door rang, alerting them that someone had entered. They stood staring at one another for a few seconds before he leaned in and gave her a solid smooch directly on the lips.

"I'll talk to you later, love. We have a lot to work out," he whispered before turning and strolling past the mortals looking at the impressive cake displays in her showroom. "She's a gem," he told them as he slipped out the front door. "A genuine angel."

Through the front window he blew her a kiss that settled in her stomach like a hot brick. Oh, this was much worse than she thought. As soon as she finished with the customers, she was going to have to find a remedy, and fast.

Two hours later, Felicity closed the last of the many volumes of magic potions and spells she'd thumbed through trying to find a way to counter the effects of the Forever Unified dust. Jutting out her lower lip, she blew, fluffing up the wispies that had escaped onto her forehead.

She was going to have to call in some favors and dust off her angel wings, but at least she had a plan. A few hours and a lot of work, and Dirk Herensuge would no longer be under the influence of her crazy magic. He could go back to his happily-ever-after with the serpent princess, and Felicity could return to her normal life of watching love happen... for everyone but her.

With a mental shake, Felicity set her chin and tightened her lips while she pushed herself up and began putting the books back on the shelves. There was no feeling sorry for herself. She'd been allowed to choose her mission, had accepted this one, and now she just needed to do it.

Slogging to the oversized refrigerator in the back of her workroom, she pulled open the door and reached in for the groom's cake with the partially decorated dragon.

One thing was certain... Felicity was a woman of her word. She took her job seriously, and quitting was not an option, especially not this far into the game.

Around the same time the next day, Adelind Chusi would become Mrs. Dirk Herensuge. They'd smile for the cameras and their guests, and slice into the cake, eating the pieces right where she'd placed the two little hearts to help them know where to make the first cut. Then they'd look at one another, a sense of euphoria falling over them both as their pupils dilated and their hearts raced, their desire for one another nearly overcoming everything else around them.

Felicity pointed a finger toward her open mouth, pretending to gag herself.

Love… She'd always taken pride in the fact that she helped make it happen. For the first time ever, that realization nearly broke her heart.

Chapter 4

Hovering outside the highest window in the West tower of Shaladorn, Felicity wished she'd kept to her last year's resolution of making sure she flew at least once a week. Even once a month would have helped. Her wing muscles were tired and, quite honestly, she couldn't wait to take the feathery extensions off. She resituated the bag slung over her shoulder and maneuvered herself around the tower to the ledge of a balcony on the same level. With a breath of relief, she touched down on the cool stone, raising her arms a second later and whispering the words that would relieve her of her wings. This would be as good a place as any to leave them while she worked her magic on the sleeping groom.

Pulling the bag free, Felicity placed it on the balcony and knelt beside it, reaching inside for the special concoction. She held the mixture above her head and circled her hands to make the particles disappear while remaining within her reach. Ever since she'd picked up the glycyrrhiza glabra, she'd been mentally reciting the magic words she'd need to say as she administered the potion. It had cost her an arm and a leg—the licorice root, not the words—not to mention the time it had taken her to find someone with an actual plant in her neck of the woods. She'd used up more favors than she cared to think about just getting to the right person.

After picking the lock on the door and sneaking inside, Felicity looked upwards, nonverbally asking for forgiveness and a little assistance in making sure her scheme worked. Otherwise, there was no way the shifter was going to be the man who fell head over heels for Adelind Chusi, until death did they part... and for a dragon and a serpent, that could be a very, very, very long time. One thing was certain, Felicity didn't wish that for either of them and that was enough to spur her forward in her mission.

Three steps in and the hair on the back of her neck stood on end. Felicity froze when something thumped behind her. It wasn't until a prolonged meow broke the silence that her heart began beating again.

"Hey," she whispered as she turned, her hand on her chest. She was beyond thankful to see a cat. She smiled when it sidled up to her and began rubbing on her legs. She loved cats. Especially friendly ones.

Squatting, she began scratching the grey and white beauty under the chin before stroking down the length of his back, and was rewarded with a series of loud purrs.

"Just one more." She spoke quietly, giving the top of his head a good rubbing. "I've got to get busy and make things right with your master before the sun comes up and the household starts getting ready for the we... wedding."

Pushing back to her full height, Felicity bit her bottom lip in an attempt to stave off tears. She refused to get upset over something she couldn't change, especially when she needed to concentrate on the one thing she could.

On angel slippers, she crept down the hall that led to

the bedroom. It was a good thing he'd pointed out his window on the Volyris castle, otherwise, there was no telling where she'd have ended up inside the walls of Shaladorn. Unfortunately, there wasn't a single sound to lead her.

Holding her breath, she peeked around the door frame, her brows shooting up. The room, bathed in moonlight, was splendid. Even in the muted light, the deep, rich corals and brilliant golds practically glowed. They must have been used as representation of his dragon. Dear Lord, he surely had to be majestic and beautiful when he changed.

She looked up, imagining him flying, and the hammerbeam ceiling nearly took her breath away. The unique layout of the decorative rafters rivaled those of the finest medieval abbeys. She nearly giggled. There was absolutely nothing else about the shifter that made her think about abbeys, though it was likely this castle had been around way back then. Still, she hadn't expected to see such exquisite design work and craftsmanship, and the height alone was awe-inspiring. Most probably, the room would easily accommodate him in dragon form. Except for the furnishings. They may have been oversized in scale, but dragon-sized they were not.

The angel let her eyes wash over everything, trying to take it all in, from the writing desk beneath one of the lower windows—which had to be the one he'd showed her on the Volyris piece, to the vast bookcases lining one wall, and the tapestry covered chaise in front of the fireplace. She noted the stone box was surrounded by a carved wood Trumaeu mantle that commanded attention. Most assuredly from the

Renaissance era, it was probably walnut, though it blended perfectly with the oak rafters overhead... and that bed! The antique, four-poster, carved wood bed was an absolute masterpiece... and it was empty.

"Impressive, isn't it?"

Felicity wheeled around to see the dragon shifter leaning against the hall wall a few feet away from her. How had he managed to get there without her knowing? She must have been more lost in her perusal than she'd thought, though she was suddenly on full alert.

Dirk chuckled when she opened her mouth to say something, anything, and no words came out.

At the sound of his laughter that made his chest ripple, Felicity's mouth went even drier than it was when it hit her that he was shirtless. Merciful heavens! Did she dare look further down?

She did, relief making her eyes flutter when the band of his bottoms came into vision. Slung low on his hips, the drawstring perfectly accentuating what lay beneath, grey lounge joggers had never looked so good.

With deliberate slowness and a crooked grin, he pushed away from the wall and sauntered toward her. A clean, masculine scent assaulted her senses, causing an explosion of tiny tendrils of pleasure to course through her body. When he reached up to touch her hair, she stiffened. She breathed in small, shaky gasps and a dull throbbing settled between her legs. She may have whimpered when he moved closer, leaving very little room between himself and the door jam.

"Kings have slept in that bed—princes and princesses

conceived there. The panels were hand carved by Riemenschneider in the early 1500s. Want to know what's on them?" When she mouthed *yes*, he smiled, his face moving closer to hers. "Dragons and angels." She gasped and he nodded. "You know what's more impressive than all that?" He raised a brow and she very slowly shook her head, her eyes never leaving his. "What can happen *in* it," he whispered, his voice growing husky as he bumped her nose with his and took advantage of the deep breath she pulled in through barely parted lips. He pressed his mouth to hers.

Felicity's knees buckled at the touch of Dirk's tongue on hers.

He tightened his hold around her waist, pulling her closer while he continued his gentle, evocative exploration of her mouth. "I could show you," he offered, pulling back but not away.

When she didn't answer, he leaned back in claiming that sensitive spot beneath her ear after a quick nibble on her lobe.

Felicity thought her lungs might quit working, and was sure her brain had when she didn't push him away. Her heart beat faster, especially when he pressed against her and she felt the hard evidence of his desire against her lower belly. Oh, she was in trouble.

Never before had Felicity wanted someone the way she wanted this man in that moment. With her nipples pressed taunt against the inside of the angelcloth gown she wore, her sex throbbing like nothing she'd ever experienced, she knew the moment of truth was upon her. She had to tell him to stop or cross the point of no return. When her fingertips raked against the hard planes of his chest, she knew there was no turning back. Instead, she ran her hands up behind his neck, snaking them into his thick, dark hair with the golden highlights.

For a few hours, Felicity would be no angel, she'd love him and let him make love to her... and then she'd administer her magic, undoing the Forever Unified potion with a little extra something to make him remember their time only briefly... make him believe it was just a dream. She could live with that, especially carrying the memory of his heart beating next to hers as their bodies intertwined and became one. She needed this. It was the only way she'd ever be able to complete her mission.

"I'd like to see." She ran her hand slowly down his chest, over the rippled muscles of his toned abdomen, and hooked her fingers into the top of his waistband to make sure there was no doubt about her intention. "I'd like to be impressed."

With dragon speed quickness, Felicity found herself transported from the doorway to the satin-topped comfort of the ancient bed with the shifter hovering above her. She felt him probing her mind for assurance, saw his relief when she briefly let him in and he found it just before she shuttered her thoughts again. He need not know the fullness of her plan—a plan she practically forgot herself as he settled beside her and his hands and mouth began to explore her body.

Face to face, chest to breasts, stomach to stomach, he kissed her, his lips moving slowly over hers, letting her know the pace their time together would take.

That was fine with Felicity. This one union would have to last her a lifetime. She hoped, no needed his every touch to be seared into her memory and onto her body in a way that she would never forget. She closed her eyes, enjoying the moment.

Dirk's mouth moved from hers to her jaw and then down to her neck, following the trail of his fingers toward the crevice between her breasts. He kissed one hard mound through the soft material that covered it, then slipped the neckline of her gown aside to expose the erect peak of the other.

If the warmth of the air radiating off them hadn't been enough to set her on fire, the heat of his mouth as he pulled her nipple past his teeth pushed her over the edge, especially when he raked his tongue over the sensitive tip before tracing the outer edge, all while his hand moved further down.

When his fingers touched her upper thigh, Felicity thought she might explode, until they begin to inch upward again, this time beneath the angelcloth hemline. She stilled, barely able to breathe, but in the best possible way.

Deft fingers stroked the edge of her lace panties, slipping beneath the flimsy material seconds before she cried out in a moan that refused to remain quiet. He answered with a growl, his finger circling the sensitive nub between her legs before joining another already probing through the glossy sheen into unexplored territory.

"Oh, angel." He breathed the words when she began to pant, her rising hips pressing her harder against his hand. Seconds later he was positioned between her legs, his mouth replacing fingers that now pushed the lacy material to the side.

"I... I ca... I can't stopppp," she stammered as his tongue assaulted her, exploring every curve and crevice of her engorged mound.

When he placed a finger against her and began to rub softly as his tongue thrust as deep into her as it could, it was obvious he had no desire for her to stop. Felicity released the fistfuls of coverlet and pushed herself up on her elbows, just enough so that she could watch. She could feel his lips curve into a smile, and was thankful the action didn't lessen his pace. Each thrust pushed her closer to a precipice she was desperate to fall over.

As her body began to shudder, she lay back, her fingers winding into his hair, her hips bucking, bringing her again and again tighter against his face. She would pay dearly for the stubble that scraped her thighs, but it was a discomfort she was willing to bear just as she was the heartache she knew would come from walking away with the morning light.

A split second of melancholy was replaced with mind blowing pleasure as her body convulsed into wave after wave of euphoria that had barely begun to subside when she found his mouth on hers, the hard fullness of him pressing at her core. Felicity had no idea where her lace panties had gone or how her gown had been removed, only that his heat burned into her through skin on skin. Direct contact. My God, she'd only ever imagined it could feel so good.

Dirk inched his way deeper, slowly allowing her time to acclimate to his size.

Felicity almost giggled as she wondered if all shifters were so wonderfully... blessed, though the elation of having him fill her overcame all other thought. In that moment, nothing else existed beyond him and her, and the very place where they were joined. *One*, she thought. As he began to move, her body picking up the rhythmic dance in its exactness, together, they melted into one... a feeling that would not stop until they'd climbed to the highest heights, not once, but three times before the first light of morning began to replace the diluted rays of the lover's moon.

"I'll have to go after this," she told him when he rolled over her once again. He nodded, the adoration in his gaze as he looked down at her another memory she would capture and store away. It didn't matter that it was caused by the Forever Unified powder. She still wanted to remember it, and she could always pretend.

"You've stolen my heart, Angel." He let out a prolonged moan as he pushed into her.

Once she could trust her voice again, she smiled and answered him with a humorous wink. "I'll give it back shortly."

Dirk chuckled, nipping at her chin. "I'd rather you just give me yours."

Felicity raised her brows, started to ask if he hadn't already claimed the heart of another, then thought better of it. This might just play right into her plan once it came time to give him the antidote to the love potion. Once they were finished, she'd put her strategy into motion.

It would be perfect.

...almost as perfect as the way her body was beginning to feel, though this time she wanted to make sure to concentrate on him, to memorize his sounds, his expressions, to truly focus on that exact moment of release, when his essence would flow into her...

She only hoped she could maintain her sanity long enough to do so. His every move had already begun to drive her crazy, bringing her closer to that wonderful abyss.

When she voiced her desire, not disclosing the full reason, it only took a second for him to accommodate her command, flipping them so that her legs straddled him, his shaft twitching as it stood straight up inside her. When she didn't start moving right away, he grasped her waist before letting his hands slide slightly lower and urging her forward and then back.

"There." He smiled as she got the hang of it. His eyes fluttered, dark lashes caressing strong cheekbones as he let out a soft moan. "You feel so good, Angel."

She nodded. There was no way he could know just how good she felt with him inside her, filling her, stretching her, stroking every sensitive nerve ending where their bodies made contact.

Focus, she reminded herself. Her task was almost unbearable until she adjusted her position, causing him to suck in several short breaths, and realized just how much control she had. Oh, she was going to have fun... wicked fun, she thought, moving her hips first to the left and then to the right, followed by a languorous swivel.

He growled, tightening his hold on her hips, forcing her to wedge her fingers beneath his grasp and push his arms above his head. Knowing how much stronger he was than her, Felicity knew, of course, that he was allowing her to have her way, especially when he bucked his hips a couple of times to pound into the farthest depths of her wet core.

"Come on, dragon man," she crooned, pressing herself up higher to where her right breast was temptingly close to his face, all the while keeping up a steady pulsating of her hips against his.

The change in her position opened her legs wider, drawing him yet deeper and he groaned when she pulled her breast away after a few seconds, greedily latching onto the other when she moved it closer. His breathing, plus the tautness of his body, not to mention the increased rigidity of his flinching cock inside her, let her know he was getting close.

Felicity desperately wanted to let go and ride the crest of euphoria with him this one last time, but she couldn't. She needed to watch him. *Focus*, she reminded herself again, chastising herself for her inability to keep her mind on her mission.

Mission… she repeated the word over and over. Missions were what angels were all about. She had hers, and at that very moment, her mission was to immerse herself in the pleasure of watching this man shatter in an explosion of pure bliss.

"Come on, baby," she whispered, increasing the rhythm. "Come on, my dragon. Let me see you fly…"

Just when she thought there was no way she could hold out any longer, he threw back his head and let out a roar that she was sure had to have shaken the windows. He pulled his hands free from hers, pressing one to the small of her back and forcing her down harder and harder as he pressed up with equal force. His other hand snaked into the hair at the back of her head and pulled her down, his mouth covering hers in breathtaking possessiveness. She could feel the heat of his essence filling her, making her heady with sheer euphoria, and yet he didn't stop until she was panting and moaning as her world shattered into a million sparkling pieces.

Only then did their pace slow, stopping with them both gasping for air for several minutes.

"Amazing," she cooed, lifting her head from where she had collapsed against his chest. "It's like magic."

He chuckled, rubbing his hand up and down her bare back. "*Like* magic? Angel, it *is* magic." He gave her behind a gentle squeeze. "That's because it was meant to be."

Felicity stilled. She could feel him twitching inside her and she was sure he could feel the same, but the serious look he gave her told her it was time to do what she'd come to do. Hoping her smile looked sincere, she pushed herself up into a sitting position.

"I have to go. But before I do, I have something for you…" If this ever got out, it would surely go down as the most awkward administration of a Forever Unified antidote in history, what with her sitting astride the man she'd just made love to throughout the night. But it had to be done. She only hoped she could remember the words.

Reciting the phrases after thinking for a few seconds, the Latin words filled the castle tower room with the angel swirling her hands in the air above her while her lover looked on with wide eyes. She brought her palms together in front of her, opening them slowly to reveal the wispy shape—a heart. He smiled.

"You asked for my heart," she whispered, nearly choking on the words. "Here," she told him, lifting her hands and gently blowing. The smoky particles came apart, much like her own heart was doing, and floated through the air toward him. He breathed in a deep, surprised breath, pulling them in. It was perfect.

Except that it wasn't. Felicity had never felt so empty as she did at that moment, even with their bodies still connected in the most intimate way possible. When his brows drew down, his gaze growing confused, she reached into the air again, flinging another substance toward him.

"Somnus," she commanded. "And when you awake, you will remember this time as nothing but a dream. Dream... Dream... Dream..." she chanted as his eyes closed and his breathing evened out.

Slowly, Felicity eased from him, allowing her eyes to travel down his body one last time. She memorized the planes and the ripples, imprinting every curve, every muscle in her mind. With a soft kiss to his cheek, she backed away, pulling the coverlet over him.

"Godspeed, my love," the angel whispered, grabbing her garments and heading toward the door she'd come in, surprised she didn't cross paths with the cat again.

She shrugged, pulling on her clothes and settling into her wings before grabbing her bag and taking flight. If she was lucky, she would get home just before the sun pushed away the last of the moonlight... just in time to begin the day of her beloved's wedding. She sighed, wondering why she'd been delusional enough to think the memories of a single night in heaven with the dragon shifter would ever be enough.

Chapter 5

Felicity heard the purr of the expensive engine as it pulled up behind her in the castle driveway, but it was the string of expletives pouring from the mouth of the exiting driver that had her straightening and turning around.

Standing beside the sleekest, blackest, most luxuriously fancy car she'd ever seen, Dirk Herensuge glared at her. He looked so ferociously angry that it made her want to climb into the back of her catering van and hide until he left. This was a side of the shifter she'd never imagined in all the times he'd come into her shop.

Was it her fault the guys hauling in the chairs and tables had made it so she'd have to wedge her van in, blocking the drive? If she hadn't, she would have had to hike a mile with a cart full of wedding cake. Okay, maybe she hadn't *had* to park there, but his little hissy fit about being unable to get to the family garage, and on his big day too... she snarled, lifting a corner of her upper lip. Good grief. Maybe the man deserved a happily-ever-after with Bridezilla after all. One thing was certain, the Forever Unified antidote had definitely worked because he sure wasn't the man she'd been with during the night.

"Better not to go there," she whispered to herself. She'd save those memories for lonely nights and cold days.

Dirk stormed past her, giving her little more than a cut-eyed glare and a ferocious growl. She waited until he'd marched up the stone walkway and was out of earshot before growling back. It made one of the table haulers chuckle, which in turn made her smile. She sighed and turned away, humming a tune that always made her happy. Life, even for those who lived practically forever, was way too short to spend it in a lovelorn doldrum.

Hefting the elaborate wedding cake with the dragon cascading up the side onto the cart, Felicity reached back into the van for the last of the supplies she'd need before hauling everything into Shaladorn's great hall. She turned back around, her eyes going wide at the sight of the groom on the other side of the cart.

He blew out a loud breath and shook his head.

"Damn it. I'm sorry. I just… there's no excuse for my poor behavior." He looked off into the distance for a few seconds, grumbling and rolling his neck when he looked back. "Can we just pretend nothing happened and start over? I think that's best for everyone."

"Uh." Felicity cocked her head, forcing her eyes out of a squinty stare. "Sure." Her brows drawing back down, she carefully slipped her hand into the one he extended.

"Dirk Herensuge," he announced. "Pleased to make your acquaintance, Ms?"

Felicity stood there for a moment, unsure whether he was being serious or pulling her leg. When he tipped his head, waiting for her answer, she decided she may as well play along. "Love," she told him. "Felicity Love."

"Ah, yes. The renowned owner of *La Boulangerie de L'amour*." He waved his free hand, pointing out her laden cart. "I've heard so much about you."

Heard? He'd done a lot more than that!

"Again, I apologize for my actions earlier. Someone will come to move the car once you're finished. Just let the man at the door know so he can get it out of your way." He smiled at her and patted the hand he still held in his. "Anyway, I'm late as it is thanks to my brother's cat. The damn thing went missing..."

"Cat?" she interrupted. "Your... brother's ca..."

He nodded, not waiting for her to finish. "Who steals a cat from a top floor of a castle tower? That just... How the hell does something like that even happen? And today of all days." He released her hand and turned away, calling back over his shoulder as he went. "Goodbye, Ms. Love. Please remember to tell the doorman to have the car moved when you're finished."

And with that, he disappeared, leaving Felicity staring at an empty doorway. At that moment, that's exactly how her heart felt. Empty. Like someone had just opened it up and walked away. He had, hadn't he? She wondered if he even remembered their night together as a dream, or if the antidote had worked so well it had also stripped that memory.

It didn't matter, she tried to tell herself before grabbing hold of the sides of the cart and beginning her trek up the path. New mission, she told herself. Get in, set up, get out, and forget. In a couple of hours or less, she would be done, her job complete so she could go home where she could lick her wounds and move on. It was too bad her potions didn't work on her because she would like to have wiped out the memory of their night forever. If she kept telling herself that, surely, she'd eventually begin to believe it.

"Hey! How long have you been here?"

Felicity whipped around, nearly dropping the marzipan leaves she was adding around the edge of the groom's cake. There stood the man of the hour, looking exactly as he had before, but with a sudden one-eighty demeanor change. His grin was contagious and she would have given him a full-on smile had he not behaved so poorly earlier, plus there was a hint of concern in his eyes. Was he really that good at masking his feelings?

"Did you find your brother's cat?" she asked, not sure what else to say.

"My brother's cat? You mean m.... Wait. How did you know..."

"Jordi? Son?"

The distinctly feminine voice interrupted from somewhere in the distance, causing him to look toward a door at the far end of the great hall. He looked back, shifting slightly from one foot to the other, a sheepish grin lifting the corners of his mouth.

"My mom." He shrugged, a bit of a nervous laugh escaping him. "I'm sure she's found at least a million other things for me to do before we get this shindig started."

"Shindig. Right." Felicity had heard weddings called a lot of things. Never that, especially by the groom.

They stood staring at each other, the silence between

them growing more awkward by the second. When they both said *well* at the same time, she tittered and he chuckled.

"So, you'll be around for a while, yes?"

Felicity shook her head. "No. I just have to finish this up and... then I need to get on my way."

He frowned a bit, nodding slowly. "I don't suppose there's anything I could do to change your mind... like offering you a seat next to the best man or something..."

"Jordi! Oh, there you are."

Mrs. Herensuge emerged through the door that Felicity presumed led into other parts of the ancient castle. Felicity still hadn't answered by the time she was halfway across the hall.

"You'd better get. She's coming at you with a look of intent."

He glanced over his shoulder again, nodded and laughed. "She'll grab me by the ear like she did when I was a kid. You have no idea how much I wanted to turn into a dragon and bite her." They laughed again as he turned to go. After just a couple of steps, he turned back. "Maybe after this is all over..."

"Son!"

The exasperation in his mother's voice stopped him.

"She's coiled tighter than the bride." He rolled his eyes, motioned that he'd call, then wheeled around to go and greet his mother, slipping a comforting arm across her shoulders. Seconds later they were walking out of the hall, heads together, conferring without so much as a parting glance.

He wouldn't call. But if he did, Felicity wouldn't be home.

Chapter 6

"What the..." Felicity stopped just inside the doorway of her little cottage. She stared at the mess strewn about the large Turkish rug that laid claim to the majority of the tiny living room. Ripped up bits of cloth were everywhere.

"Bacio?" she called her cat, not surprised when the fluffy white feline failed to answer. She reached for a strip of the cloth, her mouth dropping open when she realized it was the shredded remains of the bag she'd carried with her to the castle the night before. "Bacio!" she yelled more forcefully.

With her lips pressed tightly together, Felicity marched up the stairs, knowing exactly where she'd find that purring devil. And when she did...

For the second time, her jaw dropped. There laying in the middle of her bed with Bacio stretched out beside him, was the cat from Shaladorn.

Oh, dear Lord."

She looked at the piece of material in her hand. Hadn't she vaguely thought that her bag was unusually heavy when she'd taken off from the castle balcony? The concern had been quickly dismissed, her mind more focused on her breaking heart. The only thing she could figure was that the cat had managed to catch a few particles of the sleeping potion and been out cold in her bag until after she'd left to go set up the cakes.

Oh dear. This was bad. Bad, bad, bad. There was no way they were ever going to believe she hadn't stolen the cat... because she had!

Felicity grabbed her head as she began to pace around the room. "No, no, no," she kept repeating. What was she going to do? How could she ever fix this? There was no way she wasn't going down for this. She may as well just get in her van and...

Wait a minute. That's what she'd do. She'd let them believe the cat must have gotten outside and into her van somehow and she'd found him when she got home. It wasn't a total lie... more of a white one. That last part, at least, was true. She had found him when she got home.

She looked at the clock on her bedside table and calculated the timing of her next move. She'd gone by her shop to unload and clean up before coming home, which had put her late getting back. If she waited another hour and then called the main castle number, hopefully everyone would be at the reception and she'd get voicemail where she'd be able to tell them how she'd found the missing cat, sharing that she'd bring him home in the morning... after the newlyweds had departed for some three-month tropical island honeymoon.

She glared at the cats laying all cuddled up on her bed, envying their lack of concern for anything beyond the moment. Before she left the room, she glanced back at the big grey and white fluffball. "How did you end up in the groom's tower anyway? You should have stayed where you belonged and then neither of us would be in this mess."

He answered with a clipped mew before rubbing his

head against Bacio's and stretching out to where he could use her as a pillow. Felicity rolled her eyes and turned away. At least someone was happy.

An hour later, she'd had all the waiting she could stand. She pushed up from the couch where she'd sat staring at nothing at all while her mind wandered. Too many times, she'd had to steer her thoughts back from the night and the dragon shifter's bed. Impressive was an understatement. Her body went into instant nerves-on-end mode at the thought of his mouth and hands...

"Stop!" She couldn't keep doing this to herself. She wouldn't. It was time to make the phone call and turn in for the night. The sooner she got the Herensuge family out of her life, the better.

One ring, two, three rings... Felicity jumped when the distinctly feminine voice answered. She was silent for a few seconds, her mind trying to place the familiarity of vocal patterns. She sucked in, her hand coming up to her mouth. What was Mrs. Herensuge doing answering her own phone? She didn't think rich people ever did that.

"Hello?"

Felicity gritted her teeth when the word echoed through her phone again. She stammered for a few seconds, cleared her throat and then told the woman that the missing cat was in her possession, crossing her fingers as she told her partial lie about how she believed he may have stowed away inside her van while she was setting up the cakes.

The melodic laughter that greeted the end of her story surprised the angel and she smiled.

"If it's all right, since it's getting late, I'll just keep him here overnight and return him in the morning."

"Oh no, no dear. I wouldn't hear of it. I'll send my son by to pick him up so you won't have to bother coming clear back out here. Though you're correct. It is late and... well, boys being boys, I'm afraid they've had a bit much to drink. How about I send him by around 10 o'clock tomorrow morning? Will that work for you?"

Nodding her head, Felicity then verbalized her response, assuring the woman it would be perfect.

"Oh, his name is Kuching, in case you wanted to know," the older woman told her just before she clicked the button to hang up.

"Kucing? As in... Malay for cat?"

Soft laughter sounded through the phone line. "More like the sound a cash register makes, because he continually gets into trouble and has ended up costing us so much."

Felicity laughed as well. "He seems most content with my Bacio D'Angelo. Hopefully he will remain so throughout the night. I'll be sure to have him ready when your son comes by in the morning."

"Bacio D'Angelo... Angel Kiss. Apropos. How fitting, considering your cakes having the exquisite taste of a masterpiece that's been kissed by an angel."

Felicity froze, unsure of what to say. "Thank you," she finally managed to eke out. "I'm honored that you think so."

"Think so? I *know* so. You probably don't know this... there's really no reason you should, but I was an apprentice to Raguel." She chuckled at the sharp breath Felicity drew in. "Ah, yes. It was a very, very, very long time ago. So many centuries…"

"What happened?" Felicity couldn't keep herself from asking. "Did you get your wings?"

The woman on the line chuckled. "In a way, I guess you could say I did. Only they were in the form of those on a dragon shifter that I fell madly in love with."

Felicity sucked in so hard she almost choked. Once she was certain the young angel was okay, Mrs. Herensuge sighed.

"They're hard to resist, these dragon men, but once they have your heart, there's really not much you can do, I'm afraid." She chuckled again. "I think that goes for all men, perhaps, so be sure to guard yours until you're ready to give it away, Ms. Love."

Her cheeks heating up, Felicity thanked her for the advice, hanging up with her assurance the cat would be fine until the next morning. Laying down her phone, she plopped onto the sofa, pivoting so that her feet were up, her head on her favorite white, fluffy, faux fur pillow. She stared at the ceiling, wondering whether there was any hope that the cats would let her in her own bed, and a few minutes later, she started to doze off. Go figure. Dirk Herensuge's mother was an angel who had fallen short of earning her wings.

As she drifted into a sea of sleep, her last thought was one of wondering. If her lover was, in fact, part angel, the Forever Unified dust shouldn't have had any effect on him. The reality was, if his mother had been studying under the archangel Raguel, that meant she wasn't *just an angel*, but an angel of love. And an angel was an angel, regardless of whether she had yet to receive her wings.

Chapter 7

A loud thud, followed by the trembling of the ground had Felicity springing up from the sofa like a scared cat. She stood wide-eyed in the middle of her living room, turning in a circle as she tried to figure out what had happened.

Earthquake? Seismic activity wasn't a common occurrence in the area, nothing she'd really felt before... except on the few occasions she'd been close by where a dragon had landed. She nodded, her heart slamming against the inside of her chest.

Gulping several times to try to settle her nerves, Felicity commanded reluctant legs to take her to the front door. She pulled it open just in time to see the most breathtaking dragon she'd ever seen, the golds highlighting his shimmering coral scales looking like celestial flames.

Seconds later, the massive beast morphed back into a man of equal beauty. He sauntered toward her, his lazy grin making him look even more handsome and desirable than ever before. His eyes washing down her may as well have been his hands from the way it made her body tingle. She could already feel a certain wetness beginning to cling to her panties and cursed herself for her weakness where he was concerned.

"Wh... what are you doing here?" she stammered, when he stopped a mere foot away.

"I was told you have my cat." He chuckled when her brows shot up.

"Ah, yes. The cat… though your mother said she'd send your brother in the morning."

He scrunched his nose. "Why would she say that? It's *my* cat. Besides, Dirk is probably halfway to Kohr Haven by now, relishing the thought of being in the arms of that sharp-tongued viper of his… which I guess is okay, if you're into that kind of thing."

When Felicity just stared at him, he lifted his hands and shrugged, asking her *what* by his actions.

"Wha…" She shook her head, her eyes darting about as she tried to put his comments together. She pinched herself to make sure she wasn't dreaming and he laughed.

"Ah, little angel. I get it now. All this time, you though I was Dirk because I was the one coming into your shop with Adelind."

"And… you're not?" She cocked her head, loose blonde curls slipping over her shoulder.

Jordan reached up, running one of the curls through his fingers before tugging lightly. "That fowl-mouthed, uptight, ill-tempered… Are you kidding me? I can't believe you couldn't see a difference immediately."

Now it was Felicity's turn. She shrugged sheepishly. Truth was, there was a world of difference and she should have realized the two were not the same person. "But… you look exactly alike…"

"Twins usually do, especially when they're identical."

When she bopped herself in the forehead with her palm, the shifter burst into full blown laughter and reached for her hands.

Felicity only resisted a little when he pulled her toward him, and when she was close enough, he slipped his arms around her, drawing her tight against his chest while whispering into her hair.

"Do you really think I would have taken you into my bed knowing there would be nothing more than that one night?" He looked down at the face she turned up to him, smiled and rubbed his nose against hers. "You had my heart from the first time I walked into *La Boulangerie de L'amour.*"

When Jordan ran his lips over hers, she savored their softness, then pulled back slightly.

"So, why were you the one coming into the shop with her? I've had the bride's mother come in, sometimes her best friend or bride's maid... but never a future brother-in-law." She crinkled her nose and he laughed, and she booped his chin with the upturned tip.

Jordan shrugged. "You met my brother. He's never been one to get overly concerned with details that aren't related to business matters. Though... the oddest thing happened. Once the reception started, I mean really started—after they cut the cake and had their toast and all, you couldn't have asked for a more attentive groom. It was almost as if a switch had been flipped and he was suddenly head-over-heels in love. They were both acting rather giddy, actually, now that I think about it."

His words caused Felicity to titter and he squinted down at her, pressing his lips together. "What?"

She shook her head. "Nothing. You know how women

are about weddings…"

"After being assigned by my mother to help Adelind… unfortunately, I do." He rolled his eyes and Felicity playfully smacked his arm and he feigned hurt.

"Surely it wasn't that bad." He scrunched his face and she laughed and added, "Okay, maybe with her…"

Jordan joined her in the laughter then sobered slightly. "Ah, she's not always that way. We've known her since we were kids. And, quite honestly, I think she's the only one who would ever be willing to put up with Dirk. Even our mother gets exasperated with him… which you probably gathered by the way she was acting when she came into the great hall earlier."

When she grew serious, Jordan asked her what was wrong, the concern immediately evident in his dark eyes.

"Your mom is an angel, right?"

He nodded, confirming the thoughts she'd had as she was falling asleep. What she didn't understand was, if that was true, why had the Forever Unified she'd stirred into the cake worked on his brother?

"So… uhm, about last night…" Her face turned all kinds of red as she stammered in her attempt to see how much he really remembered. "You… you remember…"

He laughed. "Angel, you're as red as that silly little character people fabricate as the devil himself." His remark only served to deepen her blush and Jordan ran the back of his hand along one flaming cheek. "To be honest, I… I wasn't quite sure whether it was real or just a dream," he told her, moving in closer and tipping up her chin with his fingertips. Looking into her eyes, he smiled. "It felt so real, too real, but then you pushed me away when I saw you at the reception... Part of the reason I came here was because I needed to know..." He touched both of her temples with his hands before cupping her face and leaning in to softly kiss her. "And now I do."

Felicity closed her eyes, hit with the realization that she'd failed to block her thoughts. She opened them again, staring into the adoring gaze of the man who'd managed to look inside her, to see their whole night played out in the vivid detail of her memory. A moment of embarrassment hit her... and then she realized it didn't matter. She never wanted to keep secrets from him. She wanted him to know that her deepest fantasies all had him in a starring role, that she'd thought having him for just one night and then walk away would be enough... and that it had hurt far more than she'd ever imagined.

She may have pretended to have given him her heart before she left his castle tower, but the truth was, she couldn't give it to him then, because she'd done so many months before without ever intending to.

When she pushed up on her toes and very gently touched her lips to his, Jordan growled before lifting her to where her feet were off the ground. He carried her inside and pushed the door closed with his heel. Spinning them around, he leaned her against the wall and pressed himself against her.

"I don't suppose you have anything in that magic bag of yours to help me remember last night from my own perspective, do you?"

With a grimace, she shook her head. "I'm afraid my

bag has seen better days."

When he gave her a questioning glance, she pointed to the shredded bits of material on the table."

"How…" He rolled his eyes. "Kucing?" She nodded and he continued. "That cat causes more trouble than he's worth. Where is the beast anyway?"

Felicity cut her eyes upward. "I think he may have found his soulmate in a little white cohort named Bacio. Unfortunately, she is a master of mischief on her own and it seems the two have taken over my bedroom."

Jordan raised a dark brow.

"Don't worry. There won't be any mini fur balls running around in a few weeks. At least not from the two of them."

He laughed. "Believe me, the threat of mini fur balls was the farthest thing from my mind." He nuzzled her jaw just below her ear and whispered, "It was more the thought of your bedroom."

"Oh!" Her expression of surprise turned to one of pleasure as he continued an oral assault of the same area. "Oooh. Jordan…"

At the sound of her saying his name, the dragon shifter pulled back, though only long enough to remind her that if she'd said his name early on, none of this misunderstanding would have happened. He quickly took that back once he realized she probably wouldn't have had a reason to visit his tower if that had been the case. He shook his head and leaned back in, his mouth covering her, his tongue commanding entrance, which she freely gave.

"Where is this bedroom of yours?" he asked, his

breathing labored.

When she pointed at the staircase, he scooped her up and headed that direction, taking two steps at a time. At the doorway, he paused.

"I'm afraid it's not quite as beautiful as yours." She watched his face for a reaction.

Jordan looked around, a crooked smile curving his mouth. "It does look a bit like Cupid threw up, but... I kinda like it."

Felicity giggled. "Watch it! Cupid just so happens to be a friend of mine."

"Just as long as he doesn't get too friendly with my angel."

Felicity giggled. She knew she should probably be annoyed with his possessiveness, but she found it somehow endearing. He was a dragon, after all.

"He's actually quite handsome, you know. Not at all the silly cherub mortals like to make him out to be."

"Just how well do you know this," he growled, "Cupid?"

She wiggled her eyebrows and then told him she was only kidding. "He's actually my cousin, though I do hope that someday he'll get hit by his own arrow."

"The only arrow I'm interested in is…"

"Shhh!" She pressed her finger to his mouth, her face turning an instant scarlet again.

"You know you are too."

Felicity couldn't deny it, especially as the tingling in her breasts caused her to shiver. Jordan kissed her again and then walked them over to the bed. Fortunately, the cats had already moved to the window seat where they lay curled up together in Bacio's bed.

Jordan sat his angel on the edge of the bed, then knelt on the floor beside her.

Felicity watched, noting the tightness in his neck as he worked to swallow.

"I have no doubts in what I'm about to say," he told her, taking both her hands in his. "It's just... not something I ever expected. I'm not necessarily proud of it, but I figured I'd be a player the rest of my days. There was no way I'd ever envisioned myself as an actual groom." He looked from Felicity's hands to her face when she sucked in a hard breath. "But... if you'll have me, Ms. Love... I'd be honored to change your name to Herensuge."

He watched her intently, his eyes tearing up when hers did.

"Oh, don't cry, honey. It's okay. I mean, I know it might have been kind of fast to ask..."

"Jordan," she whispered, silencing his rambling. "What do you see in my thoughts?"

He stared at her for a few seconds, seeming confused before a slow smile light his face. "Yes!"

"Yes." She nodded. "Of course I'll marry you, you crazy dragon."

With a whoop, he slipped a hand to the back of her neck and pulled her face down to where he could easily kiss her.

"You have made me the happiest man... dragon... whatever..."

They both laughed as he sat back on his heels.

Looking up at her, he trailed a hand down her cheek before settling his palms on her knees. Even before he began sliding them up her legs, Felicity was already pulling in a shaky breath. When he reached the top of her panties, she lifted just enough so that he could slip them off her.

"You wore white last night, didn't you?"

She nodded, as did he before he tossed the coral colored lace to the side.

"Pretty," he said, though he seemed to have quickly lost interest in the garment, concentrating on what was beneath them.

Jordan slid her up on the bed and lay her back, stretching forward just far enough to run his tongue over the already engorged folds at the apex of her legs.

"There's no magic in the world that could make me forget this," he mumbled against her, his words causing an electrifying vibration to the very center of her core.

Minutes later, she was moaning his name, though just before she crashed over the edge, he sprung up, covering her body with his own as he buried himself inside her, mumbling his need to feel her wrapped around him, to sheathe himself in her warmth—words that had her climbing higher and higher until her body could stand no more. When she cried out against his shoulder, Jordan lifted his head, staring down at her as she came undone, her ecstasy the stimulus that pushed him to give her everything he had with a series of groans and roars and a whisper of her name.

As they lay together afterwards, her body already beginning to respond again to the casual stroking and exploration of his fingers against her skin, Jordan chuckled causing Felicity to turn dreamy eyes to stare at him. Through upturned lips, he answered a question she hadn't even realized she was thinking about, until he replied.

"Last night, when you came to the tower, I watched you fly in and thought I'd never seen such a beautiful sight..." He let his gaze slide down her. "Until now."

Fighting a blush and failing, Felicity smiled sheepishly and turned into him. "But how... I didn't see you until you were behind me in the hall?"

"Of course not. You were intent on your mission. I flew in after you, following your every move... just a few seconds behind."

"You were out flying?" she quizzed.

"I was actually on my way to see whether you might be interested in a little moonlit flight with me, but then I saw you..."

"No! That's not possible. I mean, I saw your dragon when you got here. How would I not have seen you?" She shook her head, but he just kissed her nose and nodded.

"You forget. Not only do the Druajen have the ability to read thoughts, we also have outstanding eyesight."

She smiled. "You were really coming to find me? To fly?"

"Yep." He chuckled. "And if last night was anything like tonight, boy did we ever fly."

They both laughed, their actions ending in bodies pressed closer together, mouths finding each other for another kiss.

When Felicity felt the evidence of his returning desire,

she pushed against him, pressing him to where he lay against her pillows and silly red silk comforter. She slid down his body, her tongue tasting each inch as she went.

She took him in her hands, both fists not enough to fully cover him, she was amazed he'd managed to fit inside her. Her thoughts made him laugh, though his mirth was quickly replaced by a hiss as she ran her tongue across his now fully engorged head before playfully raking her teeth along the same path. Oh, this was going to be fun.

"Fun, yes," Jordan breathed out as she slowly covered him with her mouth, his next words coming out between a series of moans.. "A lifetime of *fun*, my angel of love."

A lifetime… not a day more, not a day less. That was all a little angel could ask.

Chapter 8

Three and a half months later, Jordan inhaled and exhaled slowly, at the urging of his twin brother, in an attempt to ease his nerves. He couldn't believe he was making this leap, even though it was what he wanted, without a doubt. He'd just never, in over five hundred years, imagined himself as a good choice for the role of groom.

But Felicity had, and so had his heart. He looked down, smiling at the thought of the two hearts she'd placed on the side of their wedding cake. She'd told him it was symbolic of her heart beating next to his, and that they were the pieces they should eat first.

She hadn't fooled him. He knew exactly what she was up to. Sprinkled over that piece was an extra layer of the same dust she'd stirred into their wedding cake… the magic that was supposed to keep him forever happy at her side.

When the music started, Jordan looked up, the vision of an angel swirled in the clouds caused by the moisture droplets that sprung up in the corners of his eyes. My God, she was beautiful. With such short notice, and no real family on Felicity's side, his mother had offered to let her wear the dress she'd worn when she'd married his father. He'd seen pictures of it, of course, but he'd never imagined it could look even more beautiful… but Felicity, with her angel wings flying high, blonde curls framing her sweet face, had made the dress a masterpiece… just like her cakes… just like her, his angel.

His angel… the one being that had melted his heart and melded it with her own in a delicious recipe that was pure heaven. There'd be no need for magic to keep them together.

RECIPE: INCREDIBLY DELICIOUS
ITALIAN CREAM CAKE

CAKE MIX
1 Cup Buttermilk
1 Teaspoon Baking Soda
½ Cup Butter
½ Cup Shortening
2 Cups White Sugar
5 Eggs
1 Teaspoon Vanilla Extract
1 Cup Flaked Coconut
1 Teaspoon Baking Powder
2 Cup All-Purpose Flour

FROSTING
8 Ounces Cream Cheese
½ Cup Butter
1 Teaspoon Vanilla Extract
4 Cups Confectioners' Sugar
2 Tablespoons Light Cream
½ Cup Chopped Walnuts
1 Cup Sweetened Flaked Coconut

Preheat oven to 350 degrees F (175 degrees C). Grease three 9 inch round cake pans. In a small bowl, dissolve the baking soda in the buttermilk; set aside.

In a large bowl, cream together 1/2 cup butter, shortening and white sugar until light and fluffy. Mix in the eggs, buttermilk mixture, 1 teaspoon vanilla, 1 cup coconut, baking powder and flour. Stir until just combined. Pour batter into the prepared pans.

Bake in the preheated oven for 30 to 35 minutes, or until a

toothpick inserted into the center of the cake comes out clean. Allow to cool.

To Make Frosting: In a medium bowl, combine cream cheese, 1/2 cup butter, 1 teaspoon vanilla and confectioners' sugar. Beat until light and fluffy. Mix in a small amount of cream to attain the desired consistency. Stir in chopped nuts and remaining flaked coconut. Spread between layers and on top and sides of cooled cake.

http://allrecipes.com/recipe/7871/incredibly-delicious-italian-cream-cake/
Recommended by my friend: Author Cathy Collar

Author Note

I've said it before, and I'll say it again, books are not created in solitary. No matter how many hours one spends alone, tapping away at a keyboard, walking around talking to oneself, or staring off into the distance while trying to flesh out a scene, breathing life into a book takes a monumental number of people: And it often starts well before the first words are put on any page.

To my mom who smiled politely when I recounted, in vivid detail, something that had happened at school that day or the whole plot to a movie. She told me then that I needed to become a writer. Thanks, Mom. I did! To my siblings who always provided great fodder. Jackie and Bobbi are the only two left, but we make the most of our days together. They may not realize all the bits and pieces of our near daily conversations that get sorted away for future stories. Maybe we don't need to tell them! To my editor, Grace Augustine, for not only helping my words fit together better, but for also instilling in me the self-confidence to write the stories unfolding in my mind. You have become a true and dear friend, Grace. I'm excited to see what comes next for both of us. To Darlene Kuncytes and Andi Lawrencovna… thank you both for not only organizing the Sinfully Delicious box set that this story was originally a part of, but for making it possible for us to donate the proceeds to such a worthy cause, one that is as near and dear to my heart as the two of you. I love you both to the moon and back, just as I do my new friends found through this set: Marj Ivancic and Crystal Gauthier. Both of you are filled with such humor and talent. May we meet soon on another project. And to Julia Mills… you touch my heart on a daily basis and I am so honored to not only get to work with you as both an author and cover designer, but to also call you my friend.

I will never write a book that I don't thank two people in particular. One is Patrick Sipperly. Pat and I grew up together on the Kenai Peninsula of Alaska, graduated, and went our separate ways as so often happens to youthful friend. Twenty-five years later, we met up again, on Facebook of all places, and he asked me what I wanted to do when I grew up. My answer came easy: Write! Only that's not all I wanted, because I had dreams of seeing my words in books that others could read. His answer: Let's do it! So, we wrote a book and published it. Just like that. It wasn't a bestseller, but you know what… it happened, and it opened doors for me that I could scarcely have imagined walking through myself. For that, and for a lifelong friendship, I am forever grateful.

The other special person is Andrew E. Kaufman, writer extraordinaire. If you haven't picked up one of his books, please do yourself a favor and do so. I did, many years ago, and it not only opened my eyes to excellent storytelling, but it led to a friendship that means more to me than any bestseller ever could. Andrew is another brave soul fighting a battle on a daily basis. Myasthenia Gravis is his constant sparring partner. It's another ruthless disease that I would give anything to see defeated. Battle strong, dear friend. You are the storm.

To my Dragon Guardians… You truly are the best

group on Facebook. I seriously enjoy getting to spend time with all of you. It means the world to me, as do each of you. You are treasures that warm my heart.

And last but never least… to my readers. Thank you seems so little, but it's all I have. Thank you for loving my characters, for walking into the worlds I create, for talking about them with others, for leaving reviews… All the things you do that let me know my words and my worlds mean something. But I want to add a special thanks to all of you who purchased the Sinfully Delicious box set, because with that, you were not only loving me and my characters, but every individual helped by the American Cancer Society. For that, you have my heart.

Joining my Facebook Group is a great way to stay informed and enjoy the one on one that comes from being a part of an interactive group. You'll find Linda's Dragon Guardians at this link:

https://www.facebook.com/groups/664151640414859/

Until the next story…
Thank you for being a part of my dream,
Linda

Works by Linda Boulanger

Novels/Novellas/Novelettes
On Wings of Time
On Wings of Fire
A Leap of Faith
Arms of an Angel
Stirring Up Some Love
Heart Stones & Diamonds
A Future Full of Love
Dance with the Enemy
Beyond the Shadows
A Warrior's Christmas Gift
Makinna's Secret

Anthologies
Echoed Heartbeats
Time Out on a Roller Coaster
Becoming…
Whispered Beginnings

Color Illustrated Children's Book
When Sadie Learned to S.M.I.L.E.

Short Story Trios and Singles
Up to Bat / Center Stage / Best Friend Rules
Face of an Angel / Life Changes / Talk with Me
Secret Shame

About Linda Boulanger

Linda Boulanger is a happily-ever-after author, wife, and mother of four human children and two fur babies. She has an eclectic mix of published books, numerous story singles and short stories in a few group anthologies, plus a slew of always evolving works in progress.

Along with being an author, she designs book covers for herself and others through *Tell~Tale Book Covers* and *TreasureLine Designs*, all from her desk just north of Tulsa, Oklahoma.

Other place to find Linda:

Website
www.LindaBoulangerBooks.com

Blog
writersshelflife.blogspot.com/

Facebook
www.facebook.com/TheShelfLifeOfLindaBoulanger

Facebook Group
www.facebook.com/groups/664151640414859/

Email
lindaboulangerbooks@gmail.com

BookBub
www.bookbub.com/authors/linda-boulanger

Amazon Author Page
www.amazon.com/Linda-Boulanger/e/B002NPYDC6